Christine Doyle-Stott

WHILE THE CANDLES BURN

Eight Stories for Hanukkah

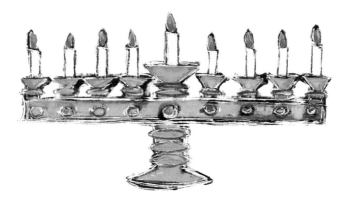

by Barbara Diamond Goldin
illustrated by Elaine Greenstein

VIKING

For Valeska and Lynton Appleberry, and Elsie and Max Canterbury, my very dear friends and lifelong mentors
—B. D. G.

For Julia, Paul, Isaac, and Shira
—E. G.

Special thanks to Rabbi Susan Freeman of Congregation B'nai Israel Hebrew School, Northampton, Massachusetts; Judith Herschlag Muffs, Judaica consultant; Rabbi Aaron D. Panken of New York City; and Dr. Jack Wertheimer, Professor of Jewish History at the Jewish Theological Seminary of America, who all read this text for background authenticity.

The illustrations are monoprints, overpainted with gouache.

VIKING
Published by the Penguin Group
Penguin Books USA Inc., 375 Hudson Street, New York, New York 10014, U.S.A.
Penguin Books Ltd, 27 Wrights Lane, London W8 5TZ, England
Penguin Books Australia Ltd, Ringwood, Victoria, Australia
Penguin Books Canada Ltd, 10 Alcorn Avenue, Toronto, Ontario, Canada M4V 3B2
Penguin Books (N.Z.) Ltd, 182–190 Wairau Road, Auckland 10, New Zealand

Penguin Books Ltd, Registered Offices: Harmondsworth, Middlesex, England

First published in 1996 by Viking, a division of Penguin Books USA Inc.

3   5   7   9   10   8   6   4   2

Text copyright © Barbara Diamond Goldin, 1996
Illustrations copyright © Elaine Greenstein, 1996

LIBRARY OF CONGRESS CATALOGING-IN-PUBLICATION DATA
Goldin, Barbara Diamond.
While the candles burn : eight stories for Hanukkah/
by Barbara Diamond Goldin ; illustrated by Elaine Greenstein.   p.   cm.
Summary : A collection of eight stories illuminating the meaning and the miracles of Hanukkah.
ISBN 0-670-85875-7 (hardcover)
1. Hanukkah—Juvenile fiction.   2. Jews—Juvenile fiction.   3. Children's stories, American.
[1. Hanukkah—Fiction.   2. Jews—Fiction.   3. Short stories.]   I. Greenstein, Elaine, ill.   II. Title.
PZ7.G5674Wh   1996   [Fic]—dc20   95-50310   CIP   AC

Manufactured in China   Set in Palatino

CONTENTS

INTRODUCTION   1

DAY BY DAY: Faith   5

AN EXTRA TWELVE: Miracles   11

LIFE IS LIKE A DREIDEL: Traditions   19

THE RIVER OF TORAH: Religious Commitment   27

SHALOM / SALAM: Peace   31

THE WOMEN'S REWARD: Honoring Women   39

A DIFFERENT STORY: Charity   45

REMEMBERING RIVKA: Rededication   49

SOURCES OF THE STORIES   59

INTRODUCTION

Hanukkah is an eight-day festival that begins on the eve of the twenty-fifth day of the Hebrew month of Kislev. This month falls in November or December of the commonly used international calendar. *Hanukkah* is the Hebrew word for "dedication" and refers to the historical basis of the holiday. In the second century B.C.E. (Before the Common Era), the Syrians—under their Greek king Antiochus IV—ruled Judea. They tried to make the Jews become more Hellenistic, more Greek, as they had.

Besides prohibiting Jewish rituals and customs, Antiochus defiled the Holy Temple in Jerusalem by placing statues of Greek gods on the altar and sacrificing ritually impure animals there. Factions within the Jewish people at this time complicated the situation. Some Jews were pro-Hellenization, and some were against adopting the Greek gods and ways. This kind of conflict continues to exist even today among Jews, as well as members of other minority groups. Should they assimilate with the larger culture, or not? And if so, to what extent?

In the town of Modin, not far from Jerusalem, the priest Mattathias and his five sons refused to bow down to a Greek idol. Instead they fled to the hills and began a guerrilla war against the Syrian army. Some say this was the world's first struggle for religious freedom.

In 165 B.C.E., on the twenty-fifth of Kislev, Mattathias's son Judah, also called "the Maccabee" or hammer, marched into Jerusalem with his army. This was three years to the day after Antiochus had defiled the Temple. Judah and his army cleansed the Temple—they repaired the walls and doors, pulled down the desecrated altar and built a new one, crushed the idols, and brought in new sacred objects, including the large seven-branched Temple lamp, the menorah.

The war against the Syrians was not yet over. That wouldn't happen for twenty-four years. But Judah was able to recapture Jerusalem and rededicate the Temple to the service of the One God. Jews were then able to worship there for over two hundred years more—from 165 B.C.E. to the time of the Temple's destruction by the Romans in 70 C.E.(Common Era)—longer than the United States has been an independent nation.

The miracle of the Maccabees's military victory of the few against the many has been overshadowed for centuries, however, by the story of another miracle associated with Hanukkah. The Rabbis of the second century C.E. told of the single jar of oil the Maccabees found in the Temple that had not been defiled by the Syrians and still had the stamp of the High Priest. But this jar contained only enough oil to burn in the Temple menorah for one day. Miraculously, this oil burned for eight days, the time needed to produce more oil to replenish the great menorah.

One of the reasons that these Rabbis emphasized the miracle of the oil rather than the military victory might have been the political atmosphere of their time. They were under Roman rule by then. To give as the reason for their celebration a successful uprising by the Jews against an outside ruler was probably considered too dangerous.

Another reason for emphasizing the miracle of the oil may be what later happened to the Hasmonean dynasty established by the descendants of Mattathias and Judah. The Hasmoneans ruled Judea for about a hundred years. They eventually became Hellenized themselves, and caused much anguish among their own people.

An explanation of why the holiday lasts for eight days can be drawn from either one of these stories. Judah himself, according to some post-Biblical writings, called for eight days of rejoicing to be held each year at this time to commemorate the cleansing of the Temple. And the eight days of Hanukkah are also linked to the miracle of the oil that burned for eight days.

It is not exactly clear how Hanukkah was celebrated in its early decades. But there is evidence that by the second century C.E., the ritual of lighting pear-shaped oil lamps made of clay, stone, or bronze on each night of the holiday was widespread. The Hanukkah lamp was placed outside the entrance of the house, so all might see and recall the miracles. In times of danger, the Rabbis said that the lamp could be placed indoors.

Today's Hanukkah lamp, also called a menorah or *hanukkiyah*, takes many different forms. One may be an exquisite golden candelabra with intricate carved designs; another, a half of a potato with nine holes; yet another, a circle of nine clay elephants. (Antiochus's army used elephants as their version of army tanks!) What is important is that the lamp have eight holes for candles—which most people use today—or oil, and an additional spot for the server, or *shammash*, that is used to light the others.

When the family gathers around the *hanukkiyah*, traditional blessings are chanted before candlelighting. Then one candle (in addition to the *shammash*), is lit on the first night of the holiday, two candles on the second night, and so on until the final night, when eight candles blaze merrily, proclaiming the miracles. Through the ages, these lights have brought hope to Jews even in the darkest times.

Today the rejoicing that Judah called for includes eating foods fried in oil. Jews of Eastern European origin eat potato pancakes, or *latkes*; those of Spanish descent eat *bourmuelos*, crispy balls of fried dough dipped in honey; and in Israel jelly-filled doughnuts called *sufganiyyot* are popular.

While the candles burn, families sing songs, tell stories, and play games. A popular Hanukkah game is played with a dreidel, a spinning top that has on its sides the Hebrew letters *nun*, *gimmel*, *hay*, and *shin*. These are the first letters of the Hebrew words that mean "a great miracle happened there." To begin the game, players put a pile of coins, peanuts, or candies in the middle. Then each player takes a turn spinning the dreidel. Depending on which letter the dreidel lands on, the player may win all (*gimmel*) or half (*hay*) of whatever is in the center, or may win nothing at all (*nun*), or even have to put something in (*shin*).

In Eastern Europe, it was traditional for children, students, and teachers to receive *gelt* (coins) on Hanukkah, to spread light and joy, and to encourage study. The poor were given food and money, as they are before every Jewish holiday. The giving of other kinds of gifts during Hanukkah is a relatively new custom.

Today in Israel, Hanukkah is a big national holiday and includes a relay race with a blazing torch. This race begins in the town of Modin, where the Maccabee revolt began. It ends in Jerusalem where the fire is used to light the giant *hanukkiyah* that stands at the Western Wall, all that is left of the Holy Temple.

In this collection of eight stories for Hanukkah, you will find that only one actually takes place during Hanukkah. Instead, each story is meant to portray one of the many themes of the holiday—such as religious freedom and commitment, faith, courage, charity, rededication, honoring women at Hanukkah, lights, and miracles. And so the emphasis of this collection is not on how we celebrate the holiday, but on *why* we celebrate it, as we have for the past 2,100 years.

What is Hanukkah? We answer this question with stories that talk about its meaning as well as its miracles.

DAY BY DAY

"Day by Day" is a story about faith and the courage to live by that faith. It is about a poor man who, each day, says, "Blessed is God."

The Maccabees had to have faith to fight against the much more powerful Syrian army. And all through the centuries, Jews have had to have faith to fight persecution and live in the ways of the Torah.

In many ways, Hanukkah is about fighting for the right to be different. It is about the right not to be forced to blend in with the larger culture. Many people believe that Hanukkah celebrates the world's first fight for religious freedom.

Although Hanukkah is about a military victory, it is also about a spiritual victory. In I Maccabees 3:19, Judah the Maccabee says, "Victory in war does not depend on the size of the army, but on the strength that comes from Heaven." And in the selection from the Books of the Prophets read in the synagogue on Hanukkah, the prophet Zechariah says, "Not by might and not by power but by My spirit alone, says the Lord" (Zechariah 4:6).

There was a king long ago in Persia named Shah Abbas who was known to be an honorable and just ruler. Each evening he disguised himself so that he could wander about the streets of his city and learn more about his subjects.

Once, on the outskirts of the city, he noticed a poor hut. When he peered through the window, he could see a man sitting at the table before a simple meal, singing praises to God.

The king knocked and asked, "Is a guest welcome?"

"A guest is a gift from God," said the man. "Please, sit down and join me."

And so the king sat down. The man shared his food with Shah Abbas, and they talked of this and that.

The king asked him, "How do you earn your living?"

"I am a cobbler," answered the man. "All day long, I walk through the city streets mending people's shoes. At night, I buy my food with the money I've earned."

"And what about tomorrow?" asked Shah Abbas.

"I don't worry about that," said the man. "Just like the psalm, I say, 'Blessed is God, every day, day by day.'"

The king was impressed with what the man said and sat with him for a long time, enjoying his conversation. When he got up to leave, he said, "I will come again tomorrow."

The king wished to test this man who so impressed him. So the next day he proclaimed a new law which said: No man shall repair shoes without a permit.

That night when Shah Abbas wandered through the city streets to the poor man's hut, he was surprised to find the man eating and drinking and singing God's praises as before.

When Shah Abbas knocked on the door, the man welcomed him.

"A guest is a gift from God," he said, and shared his food with the king.

They talked of this and that, and then the king asked, "What did you do today?"

"Well, because of the king's decree, I couldn't repair shoes," the man answered. "So I drew water for people instead, and at night I was able to buy my food."

"And what will you do if the king forbids the drawing of water?"

"I will say, blessed is God, day by day," said the man, and the two continued to talk late into the night.

The next morning the king wished to test the man even more, so he prohibited the drawing of water without a permit.

That night he disguised himself once again and returned to the poor man's hut.

But just as before, the man was at his table, eating and singing praises to God.

"What did you do today?" asked Shah Abbas. "I heard that the king prohibited the drawing of water."

"I chopped wood," said the man. "And thus I earned my daily bread."

"And if tomorrow wood chopping is prohibited?" the king asked.

"Blessed is God, day by day," said the man, with not the least sign of worry on his face or in his voice.

The next morning, the king issued a proclamation that every woodchopper was to be recruited into the king's guard.

The man who was a cobbler, then a water drawer, and then a woodchopper went to the palace, where they gave him a sword and a place to stand guard. When night came, they gave the man no money with which to buy his dinner. So he gave the blade of the sword to the shopkeeper in return for some food, and went home. There he fitted a blade made out of wood into his sword hilt, covering the wood with his sheath.

Soon after, Shah Abbas came, and ate and talked and asked, "What have you done today?"

The man told him about the sword and the food.

The king said, "What if there is an inspection of the swords tomorrow? What will you do?"

"Blessed is God, day by day," said the man, and looked no more worried than the day before. Then he and Shah Abbas spent another pleasant evening together.

The next day, the captain of the guard called the cobbler to him. "The king has asked that you take a prisoner who has been sentenced to death, and behead him."

"In my whole life, I have never killed a man. I cannot do this," said the cobbler.

"It is the king's order," said the captain, and stared fiercely at him.

The man lowered his eyes. What was he to do? He repeated the psalm softly to himself. "Blessed is God, every day, day by day." And then he brightened with an idea.

"The king's order, of course," he said aloud.

The man grabbed his sword in one hand and the sheath in the other. Before all the people who had assembled to watch the execution, he said, "Almighty God, You know that I am not a murderer. If this prisoner is guilty, let my sword be one of steel. But if the prisoner is innocent of this crime, let the steel blade turn to wood."

On saying this, he drew the sword, and behold, it was made of wood! All those who stood by were amazed.

The king called the cobbler to him and embraced him. He told the cobbler of his disguise and of how he had tested him.

"I have never met a man of such faith as yours," the king told the cobbler.

And this is how the cobbler who was a water drawer and then a woodchopper and then a king's guard became the king's advisor.

AN EXTRA TWELVE

Hanukkah is a time for proclaiming miracles. Some miracles that we witness or hear about come directly from God, like the miracle of the parting of the Red Sea and the miracle of the oil that burned for eight days instead of one. And sometimes people bring about miracles by their actions, their goodness, and their faith. This was true of the Maccabees, who fought a courageous war against a great army for religious freedom. It is also true of the couple in this story, Jacobo and Esperanza, who, in serving God, help keep Avraham and his family alive.

Jacobo was a newcomer to the Holy Land. It was the early sixteenth century, and he and his wife, Esperanza, had fled the persecution of their people in Portugal. Here in this city of mystics called Safed, they could pray in a synagogue in public, instead of in a secret hide-away as they had had to do before.

Being a newcomer, Jacobo did not speak Hebrew very well and could not understand everything his new rabbi said. But one of the rabbi's talks especially touched him. It was about the ancient custom of bringing twelve loaves of bread to the Holy Temple each week before the Sabbath, as an offering to God, a custom which ended with the destruction of the Temple.

This is something we can do, Jacobo thought, *even though we are poor and do not have very much to give.* He went home and talked it over with Esperanza.

"If you can manage to buy the extra ingredients that we will need," Esperanza said, "then I will be glad to bake the additional loaves."

The very next Friday, Jacobo bought flour and eggs, sugar and oil. Esperanza prepared the usual two *hallot*, the braided Sabbath breads, for their table and an extra twelve for their offering to God.

She mixed and kneaded and baked with especial loving care so that the loaves would be worthy. Early on Friday afternoon, Jacobo wrapped them in a clean white cloth and hurried to the synagogue before anyone else would be there.

He stepped inside quietly. Looking this way and that, he tiptoed up to the wooden Ark that held the Torah scrolls and opened it. Just as quietly, he slipped the still warm and fragrant *hallot* among the Torah scrolls, and whispered, "God, we hope You will accept and enjoy this gift. Esperanza and I worked very hard to make You the very best *hallot*. You will see." Then he closed the Ark and left.

Now Jacobo did not know this, but every Friday before the Sabbath began, Avraham, the synagogue attendant, came in to sweep and clean the synagogue. This Friday afternoon, too, he came, just after Jacobo left.

Avraham was not happy. He loved his job of caring for the synagogue and doing God's work. But he did not earn enough to feed his family. Soon he would have to look for another job.

Avraham thought of his problem as he swept and dusted and put books in order. Then he went up to the Ark to pull the curtains aside so he could look at the Torah scrolls and speak of his problem before God.

But when he opened them, he spotted the white cloth and smelled a wonderful fragrance. His prayers had been answered. There before him was a gift from God! As he unwrapped the cloth, he counted one, two, three . . . twelve loaves of the most beautiful *hallot* he had ever seen. Avraham hurried home with enough bread to feed his family for the whole week.

The next morning, a very nervous Jacobo and Esperanza walked to the synagogue for the morning service. In a little while, when the Ark was opened, they would find out if God had accepted their offering. Would the cloth package they had left still be there or not? they wondered.

They sang and prayed with the rest of the congregation. Finally the moment came when they all stood and the rabbi opened the Ark. Joy filled the couple, for there was not a trace of their gift. Not even a crumb was left, Jacobo noticed, when he crept up close to the Ark to peek in while the Torahs were being carried around the synagogue.

Now every Friday, at the same time each week, Esperanza baked the loaves and Jacobo brought them to the synagogue as their gift to God. Also each week, always at the same time, Avraham dusted and swept and straightened the synagogue. And then he opened the Ark to accept the miraculous gift that waited there for him from the Holy One. This they did for thirty years.

Then one Friday, after Jacobo placed the *hallot* in the Ark, and while he was drawing away, he felt a bony old hand touch him abruptly on the shoulder.

"And what do you think you are doing?" came the voice of the aging rabbi.

"Bringing our gift to God," Jacobo explained.

"What? Bread?" demanded the rabbi.

"You told us once, Rabbi, in your sermon many years ago, about the loaves of bread that were brought to the Holy Temple every week and placed before God."

"But, Jacobo, you know very well that God does not eat! God does not have a mouth and teeth . . ." sputtered the rabbi.

"Please, Rabbi, God does eat," answered Jacobo. "I know. For thirty years, God has been eating Esperanza's *hallot*."

Just then, they heard a sound. It was Avraham arriving to clean the synagogue. The rabbi motioned for Jacobo to follow him, and they hid behind a bench to watch what happened next.

Avraham swept and straightened, and when he was done, he opened the Ark and took out the loaves.

The rabbi jumped up and startled poor Avraham. "Do you know that because you take these loaves each week, this man believes that God eats just as we humans do! All these years, he thought it was God who was accepting his gift, not just Avraham, a poor synagogue attendant."

"But, Rabbi, without these loaves my family and I would have starved," cried out Avraham. "And I thought they were a gift from Heaven, not from Jacobo."

Before the rabbi or Jacobo could reply, a messenger came hurrying into the synagogue requesting their presence before the Ari,

Rabbi Isaac Luria, one of the great mystics of Safed.

"I could hear you three arguing," the Ari told the rabbi and Jacobo and Avraham. "There is really no need to do so."

The Ari turned first to the rabbi. "Do not be alarmed by what has gone on in your synagogue these thirty years." The Ari explained: "Since the destruction of the Temple, the Holy One has not had such joy and satisfaction as was brought every Friday by Jacobo and Esperanza's innocent gift of *hallot*. That is why you yourself have lived such a long life, since it was you who inspired Jacobo.

"And you," the Ari turned next to Jacobo. "You know now who has been eating Esperanza's *hallot*. Yet do not let that stop you. Esperanza must still bake and you should still bring those twelve beautiful *hallot* to the synagogue every Friday. But now you may give them directly to Avraham. The Holy One will be just as pleased as when you placed them in the Ark itself, believe me."

"In this way, Avraham," the Ari now said to the synagogue attendant, "you and your family will still enjoy the *hallot* all week long and you can continue to care for the synagogue for as long as you are able."

And so things went on as before. Esperanza baked the *hallot* and Jacobo brought them to the synagogue. But instead of placing them in the holy Ark, Jacobo gave them into the hands of a grateful Avraham. And so the Sabbath day continued to be a joy for all—for Jacobo and Esperanza, Avraham and his family, for the rabbi, the Ari, and the Holy One on High.

LIFE IS LIKE A DREIDEL

"Life is Like a Dreidel" is based on a story by the Yiddish writer I. L. Peretz (1852–1915). This story has the flavor of the holiday traditions among the Eastern European Jews of the early 1900s. And it emphasizes the importance of lighting the Hanukkah lamp and of keeping the old traditions alive even as things change and spin in our lives.

Hanukkah traditions vary among Jews from different countries. For example, some communities in the Middle East have public feasts on Hanukkah. The most important one is for the children of the schools. All during the holiday, the students and teachers collect contributions for the feast from each household—beans, oil, garlic, onions, rice, flour, coal, and money—and then they feast and celebrate on the eighth day.

And in old Venice where many of the streets are actually canals of water, families would get into gondolas on the last night and stop in front of each house where there was a Hanukkah lamp to call out greetings and sing Hanukkah melodies.

But Jews everywhere do one thing that is the same. They all light some sort of Hanukkah lamp each night of the holiday—to publicize the miracles.

On Hanukkah, we spin the dreidel round and round and round and hope that—with luck—it will fall on the letter *gimmel*. Then we take all.

The world, too, spins round and round like a top, a dreidel. And we never know how our luck in life will fall. Will we be rich or poor? Wise or foolish? Respected or slandered? Or maybe rich one day, poor the next. Who knows?

Life is just like the dreidel. And just like the dreidel with a central point on which it turns, life's spinning motion comes from a central source, too—the Almighty. One must not forget that, as Hindy's mama and papa once did.

But why are we talking about dreidels? This story I'm going to tell you is not about dreidels. It's about a Hanukkah lamp. And not a fancy Hanukkah lamp. Not one made of silver and gold. Just a little brass Hanukkah lamp, and a broken one at that. Passed down from so many parents to so many children that it was a little bit twisted and leaned to its side. You could barely tell there were lions carved at its base or birds singing in its trees. But listen carefully and you will see how all this about dreidels fits into the story about Hindy and the Hanukkah lamp.

To start with, Hindy's family was poor. She had a mama and a papa and a little brother named Mottel and not a whole lot else. Hindy's papa bought some of this and sold a little of that. That was how he made his living. But as things change and spin, Hindy's papa bought some old iron bars from a soldier for a few pennies. After cleaning the bars, her papa saw that they shone like gold. They *were* gold!

And everything began to turn around for Hindy and her family. First, her mama and her papa threw all the old things out—the furniture, the clothes, the books. They stripped the house bare and bought all new, fancy things.

"This old junk won't do for us anymore," said Papa.

Mama took Hindy and Mottel to the fancy dressmaker's and tailor's to order some fine new clothes. And to a real barber for a haircut. Hindy hardly recognized herself or her papa or her mama or even Mottel!

And one day, Papa took the children out of their old tiny schools in their teachers' houses and into new schools. Hindy had to walk all alone to her school. None of her friends could afford to go there. Even worse, her friends would barely talk to her; they were so jealous of all her expensive new things.

And as for her brother Mottel, his new school had so many classrooms that he was forever getting lost. Not only that, he couldn't pull pranks with his friends, so he was forever falling asleep. *Rap, rap* went the teacher's ruler on his poor knuckles to wake him. Whenever Hindy saw his red knuckles, she knew.

At home, it was no better. Hindy could barely sit on the new fancy furniture. The chairs with gold braid and twisted little legs on wheels ran away with her.

Papa had no time for anything anymore, not even the holy books. He was always running here and there for "the business."

And Mama stopped fattening Hindy and Mottel up with her apple cakes and honey cookies. Nor did she read to them from her Bible anymore. She was busy having ladies to tea. And the new hired cook! She wouldn't let them near "her" kitchen.

But the world is always spinning in cycles, just like a dreidel. (See, this is where it fits in!) And before too long, everything began turning upside down for Hindy's papa.

The business floundered. The bills piled high. And Hindy's family was poor again.

Hindy and Mottel went back to their old schools. Their new clothes grew a little shabby and their hair long and curly. Papa and Mama went back to their old ways, too. Papa bought some of this and sold a little of that and spent more time with the holy books, which he borrowed from the rabbi. Mama went back to cooking for them and feeding them and reading the stories in her Bible.

Hindy was happy. Mottel, too. But Papa and Mama were not. They looked sad and weary and worried.

Soon it was Hanukkah, and Hindy bought some Hanukkah candles with the money she earned running errands in the marketplace. But there was not enough money for a new Hanukkah lamp.

"We must have thrown our old one out," sighed Mama. "It was broken, like all of our old things."

Then Hindy remembered Papa throwing the old broken Hanukkah lamp on top of the oven.

When Mama was out in the yard, Hindy whispered to Mottel, "Pssst. Help me."

Quietly, Hindy put a chair on top of a table and she and Mottel pushed and shoved it over to the oven. Hindy climbed on top of the rickety pile of furniture while Mottel held the chair to the table.

Hindy found lots of things there above the stove and threw them all down to Mottel: dented old wine cups and silverware, chipped saucers and ancient playing cards, and—to their great joy—the broken Hanukkah lamp! Oh how dirty everything was. Months and months of dust and dirt.

They called Mama inside to see.

"You imps!" she said with a grin. "What have you found? And I thought we had thrown it out!"

Mama took out the polish and they worked on the lamp. Even though one of the candleholders was twisted and leaned to its side, the lamp still looked beautiful. The lions carved at its base laughed, and the birds in its lush trees sang with the joy of the holiday.

Every night, Hindy and Mottel, Mama and Papa gathered around the little lamp, chanting the blessings and lighting the lights, singing the songs and spinning the dreidel.

And then it was the eighth night. They gathered around their lamp again, but this time their singing was interrupted by a knock on the door. Who could it be?

Hindy went to open it, and Baruch, a man who bought things from Papa, walked in.

"What is it?" Papa asked. "We are lighting the Hanukkah lights."

"I'm sorry," Baruch said. "But I have a crazy man here and I know how you need money. He's from a big city, in England no less, and you won't believe this—he buys broken-down things for high prices. All kinds of things. Should I bring him in?"

"I'm sure we can find something to show him," said Papa. "A broken chair? A—"

Meanwhile the Englishman walked right in. He caught sight of their little crooked Hanukkah lamp on the table, the dented old wine cups and silverware, the chipped saucers and ancient playing cards and wanted to buy them all. Just like that!

"I told you he was crazy," whispered Baruch.

They sold him everything but their broken little lamp. After all, it was still Hanukkah and the candles were still burning.

The Englishman paid them handsomely for their old things.

Why, they did not know. But we do. They were bound for a glass case in a London museum!

And, as the world spins round and round and things turn round, the Englishman's coins proved lucky. Papa's business grew, and they were rich once again. But this time, Papa and Mama did not throw everything away. They kept the old things and the old ways with the new. And as for the Hanukkah lamp—well, they kept it polished and shining bright. Even when it wasn't Hanukkah.

THE RIVER OF TORAH

This story, "The River of Torah," concerns a theme that is also very strong in the celebration of Hanukkah, that of religious commitment. Both Mattathias in the Hanukkah story and Rabbi Akiva in this story risked their lives to follow Jewish laws and customs that were outlawed by the rulers of the land. For Akiva the ruler was Hadrian, a Roman emperor, and for Mattathias, almost three hundred years earlier, the ruler was Antiochus, a Syrian. Both Mattathias and Rabbi Akiva bravely fought against assimilation into the larger culture and worked for religious and political freedom; both feared that adopting the Greek or Roman ways would lead to the death of the Jewish people.

Rabbi Akiva did not form a guerrilla army in the hills of Judea as Mattathias and his sons did. He "fought" the Romans mainly by teaching words of Torah. Studying Torah, he was convinced, would lead to a life of practicing Torah and good deeds. Eventually, Akiva became a martyr and died at the hands of the Romans for what he believed.

Long ago, during the time of the Roman rule over the land of Israel, the Jewish people were forbidden by the Emperor Hadrian to practice their religion. They could not study the Jewish teachings called Torah or observe the Sabbath or recite their prayers. Disobedience was punishable by death.

One of the most famous Jewish teachers of this time was Rabbi Akiva. Despite the Roman decrees, he still gathered the people together to study the holy words. For he believed that study leads to the practice of good deeds and to a life rich in the ways of the Torah.

Another sage, Pappus ben Judah, came to Rabbi Akiva one day while he was teaching some of his disciples.

"You shouldn't be teaching Torah in public like this," Pappus ben Judah said. "If the Roman government finds out, you and all your students will be killed."

"I am sorry, Pappus ben Judah, but I do not agree with you," Rabbi Akiva answered. "Let me tell you a story; if you listen, you will see why."

Then Rabbi Akiva began. "Once a sly fox was walking by the banks of a river. He noticed large groups of fish going from one place to another, their scales glinting as they darted about in the light of the sun.

"The fox's stomach grumbled at the sight of all that tasty fish. *Ah hah*, he thought, *lunch.*

"The fox bent down over the bank and called to a group of fish. 'Why are you rushing about so?' he asked them.

"'To escape the nets of the fisherman,' they answered. 'We must be quicker than they!'

"'You have no need to fear,' answered the fox. 'Just come up here on the dry land and stay with me. Then you will be safe from the fisherman's nets.'

"The fish did not hesitate with their answer. 'We may be fish and not sly foxes, but we are not fools. This water is our home. If we went up onto the dry land away from the water, we would not be able to live. We would surely die.'

"We are just like the fish," Rabbi Akiva said to Pappus ben Judah. "The life of Torah is for us like the water is for the fish. If we were to leave the life of Torah, which nourishes us and keeps us alive, to enter the dry land of the Romans, how much worse off we would be."

Then the Rabbi turned away from Pappus ben Judah, who could not think of one more word to say. Once more Akiva faced his students to continue the study of the holy words from the river of Torah.

SHALOM / SALAM

Jewish people, like people everywhere, long to live with their neighbors in peace. And even though the holiday of Hanukkah commemorates a military victory, there was a Hanukkah custom, little known in the United States, that centered on the themes of reconciliation and peace. In Salonika, Greece, and in other parts of the world, people who had been arguing were brought together on Hanukkah for a meal of reconciliation.

This original story is about working toward peace and reconciling differences between two boys, one Arab and one Jewish, in a school setting. Although the story is fiction, there is actually a bilingual school in Israel called Neve Shalom/Wahat al-Salam, meaning Oasis of Peace, where Jewish and Arab students learn together. Students are separated only for religious studies, and for arithmetic (because equations are worked from left to right in Arabic but right to left in Hebrew). The school is part of a community of the same name where Jewish and Arab families live together.

Shlomo was almost at the goal. It would mean so much to score a point now, at this new school. And with his team losing 0 to 1.

He lifted his foot to kick, but just then someone shoved against him hard with his shoulder and stole the ball, dribbled it away. It happened so fast. The referee blew his whistle. That was it. The game was over.

Shlomo, down on the ground near the goal, scanned the not-so-familiar faces for the boy who had shoved him. *That's him*, Shlomo thought. *That Arab kid, Ibrahim, holding the ball over his head, gloating. It figures it would be one of them.*

He got up and heard Roni, the boy who showed him around on his first day, call to him, "Are you okay?" Roni ran up to him and patted him comfortingly on the shoulder.

"Yeah. I'm surprised the referee didn't do something."

"That's soccer," said Roni.

Yeah. And the referee is an Arab, too, thought Shlomo, but he didn't say anything.

Shlomo didn't say much to Roni all the way back to the school. He was too mad. And lonely. He hated this new school, half Arab, half Jewish. Why couldn't he be back at his old one in his settlement near Tel Aviv? And just because his parents thought it would be a good idea for him to meet Arab students as well as Jewish ones and get to know both. To help the peace process, they said. Well, why didn't *they* go to school with the Arabs then, not him?

He and Roni were the last ones inside the building. Their two teachers greeted them at the door.

"Shalom," said Miriam.

"Salam," said Ahmed, the soccer coach.

There it was again. Everywhere he went here. Hebrew and Arabic, Arabic and Hebrew.

Shlomo mumbled something and looked down at the floor.

"Good game," said Ahmed.

Sure, for you, Shlomo thought.

Ahmed beckoned him to an empty seat for the first lesson of the day, right next to the Arab kid Ibrahim. Shlomo couldn't believe it. This was getting worse and worse. Now he had to sit next to the kid.

All he could think of was his friend Noam's warning. "Don't turn your back on an Arab. You'll get a knife in it. Remember all those kids who were blown up by that Arab terrorist on that school bus last year?"

Shlomo slid all the way over to the edge of his seat farthest from Ibrahim. He looked around for Roni and spotted him, seats and seats away.

It was a stupid lesson called family history.

"First we'll draw our family trees and then later we'll share them and stories of our families with the class," said Miriam in Hebrew.

And Ahmed in Arabic.

Everything takes twice as long here, thought Shlomo. *Arabic and Hebrew, Hebrew and Arabic.*

I can't learn this way, he thought. *Only three days here and already I'm desperate for my old school. Maybe if I do badly enough, my parents will have to take me out.* But then he felt a pang of guilt. He knew how disappointed they'd be.

He could just hear his father. "If Arabs and Jews get to know each other, we won't be so afraid of each other and hate one another. We've got to start somewhere. And this school is a start. Very few Jews have the opportunity to go to a school with even a few Arabs, let alone one like this one that is half Arab and half Jewish."

Yeah. Some opportunity, Shlomo thought.

They spent the rest of the morning in math groups. He got to sit next to Roni, and Ibrahim was way over on the other side of the room. No pushing for now.

Just before lunch, they all went to their lockers. Shlomo fumbled through his backpack and groaned. Well, going to a new school hadn't helped his memory any. His lunch was at home, right where he'd left it. Now what was he going to do? If he were at his old school, he would have had no worries. Noam or Elie or Dan always shared their lunches with him. But he wasn't at his old school.

At the lunch table, when Roni asked him where his lunch was, Shlomo pretended that he wasn't hungry. He felt too embarrassed to admit that he'd forgotten it. Instead he took out his colored pencils and some paper and drew while the others ate and talked—in Arabic and in Hebrew, of course.

He doodled at first. After a while, the doodle looked like a guitar, like the one he wanted for his thirteenth birthday. So he drew a better one that looked exactly like the guitar in the window of the music store in Tel Aviv. Shlomo sat back, pleased with the drawing. Then he felt someone staring at him. Shlomo jerked his head quickly to the right and caught him. It was Ibrahim. He gave the Arab kid a fierce look.

He's probably planning what he'll do to me in the next soccer game. Or sooner, Shlomo thought grimly.

Finally, lunch was over, and then Shlomo had to sit through *actualia*, current events. Everybody else was talking about sports and elections and peace agreements, and all Shlomo could think of was that big empty feeling where his lunch should be. He still had to live through English and science before he could get on the van for the long ride home. Home—where he felt comfortable. Where there were no Arabs right next to you, staring at you. Where there was lunch on the kitchen counter.

Before English class, Shlomo went out to get his textbook. He stopped abruptly in front of his locker when he saw it. A bulging paper bag. He looked around nervously. It wasn't his. Should he touch it?

Gingerly, he poked at it with his pencil. It was soft and squishy. He straightened up and sighed. *Come on, Shlomo*, he said to himself. *Aren't you carrying this a little too far?*

He took another deep breath, reached for the bag, and opened it. It exploded—with a sandwich, a delicious-smelling pita sandwich filled with hummus and tomatoes and cucumbers. Shlomo leaned back against the wall, relieved, and grinned.

Someone had given him a sandwich. But who? Roni? Yes, that was it. It was Roni, who could run home and fix one up for a starving fellow soccer player.

Shlomo took a bite of the sandwich. Boy, did it taste good. He was wolfing it down when he heard Miriam calling him. He dashed back to class, slipping into a seat just as she started the lesson.

"Today we will read, in English of course, about the Wright brothers, who flew the very first airplane."

Shlomo tried to get Roni's attention, to thank him, but Roni never turned around.

The lesson was interesting, so at first Shlomo didn't notice the note. It was folded neatly in quarters and lay on the side of his desk.

He smiled. *Roni*, he thought.

Shlomo opened the note. In perfect Hebrew it said, *I know you're mad about the goal. So I saved you my sandwich. Okay?* It was signed *Ibrahim*.

Shlomo sat motionless in his seat. *It was Ibrahim? I ate his sandwich? Oh no. I've probably been poisoned.*

He glanced at Ibrahim, who was sitting across the aisle. Ibrahim was smiling, a friendly smile. Definitely a friendly smile. The first smile Shlomo had seen on his face.

Shlomo looked down at the note and read it again. *Could he really have saved me his sandwich? And all this time I thought he shoved me on purpose and was planning more, much more.*

Shlomo sat there, puzzled, trying to sort out this new school, with its Arab students and Jewish students, its Jewish teachers and Arab teachers. He looked at Ibrahim again and couldn't help but smile. "How do you say 'Thanks for the sandwich' in Arabic?" he whispered.

THE WOMEN'S REWARD

This story told by Rabbis long ago gives one explanation of why the monthly holiday of the New Moon, Rosh Hodesh, has for thousands of years been singled out as a women's holiday.

This story is included here because Rosh Hodesh always falls on the sixth night of Hanukkah, ushering in the Hebrew month of Tevet, which follows Kislev.

There are two famous stories about women told during Hanukkah, both from the Apocrypha (books written around the time of the Bible, but not included in the Hebrew Bible). One is about Hannah and her seven sons, who refused to obey Antiochus, and died rather than give up their Jewish ways. This story can be found in chapter seven of the Second Book of Maccabees.

Another is the legend of Judith, who fed the Assyrian general Holofernes salty cheese so that he would drink a great deal of wine to quench his thirst. Then, after the wine made him fall asleep, she killed him, thus saving the Jewish people from the Assyrian army's siege of their city. Judith's story is the basis for a tradition of eating dairy foods on Hanukkah. The historical connection between Judith's story and Hanukkah is not exactly clear. Some scholars believe that her story, in the Book of Judith, may have been written in the days of the Maccabees to inspire courage.

Special customs involving women and Hanukkah include one in Tunisia, where Rosh Hodesh Tevet is called "the New Moon of the Daughters." Husbands and parents give gifts to wives and daughters then.

In North Africa, the seventh night of Hanukkah is dedicated to women. They fill the synagogue that night. Usually these women are not allowed to take the holy Torah scrolls from the Ark, but on this night it is their privilege to do so. They kiss the scrolls joyously, pray, and then sing and dance.

Another custom in some communities is that women do not work while the Hanukkah lights are burning. In some places, women did not work for all eight days of the holiday, to commemorate their bravery during the Maccabean period.

Thousands of years ago, the Jewish people were slaves in the land of Egypt. Then God heard their pleas, and through the leadership of Moses and the working of miracles, led them out of Egypt. Ahead of Pharaoh's chariots they went, across the Red Sea to a new life as a free people. But this freedom, which brought uncertainties and trials, as well as an end to their oppression, was not always easy for the former slaves. And so some wished for what they knew back in Egypt and their life as slaves.

One especially difficult time for the former slaves was after the Red Sea crossing, after the people began their wanderings in the desert in search of the Promised Land. They were encamped at the base of Mount Sinai, waiting anxiously for their leader Moses to return from the mountaintop. He had promised he would bring with him the words of God that would tell them how they should live as a free people.

It was a long forty days and forty nights that they waited for their leader. The people grew more and more fearful in this strange place. Some doubted that Moses would ever return.

And they complained: "The Egyptians can see their gods, carry them about, dance before them, sing to them.

"Aaron, brother of Moses, make a god we can see and pray to," they cried. "Like the ones the Egyptians have."

"Patience," pleaded Aaron. "Moses will return. You will see."

But many of the people had no patience. They grew yet more fearful and felt more lost.

Aaron did not know how long he could wait. He remembered how a group had killed the righteous Hur when he tried to remind them of all the miracles the One God had performed for them.

He searched the faces of the multitude before him and noticed that the women stood apart and did not cry out for the false god, the idol.

I will try to gain some time for my brother's return, Aaron thought. He called out loudly. "I will do as you wish and make the golden god."

Immediately the crowd hushed.

"But it must be the women who give me their jewelry from which to create this statue."

The women refused, as he had hoped.

"Our husbands and fathers and sons think God has forgotten them," one woman cried. "But it is they who have forgotten God."

The men were shamed into silence. For a time.

Yet when Moses still did not appear on the path that led down from the mountain, the fear grew again.

"He is lost to us," some cried out once more.

And this time the men, who also wore earrings, in the style of the Egyptians, pulled off their gold earrings and threw them at Aaron. They forced him to build the idol, a golden calf—all except for the men of the tribe of Levi.

It was then, as the idol builders danced and sang around the golden calf, that Moses appeared on the mountain path. Against his shoulder he carried two stone tablets with God's words, the Ten Commandments, etched on them. His gaze was radiant yet peaceful, until he saw the Israelites and their golden calf. In his fury at what his people had done, he threw down the sacred tablets and they shattered into pieces at the base of the mountain.

Many were punished that day, and the golden calf was destroyed. But one group was rewarded in a particular way. For their determination not to forget the One God and participate in the building of the golden idol, the women were given a holiday for all time.

On this New Moon holiday, when the moon is at its beginning, women are given a chance to renew themselves as well, in spirit and in energy. In olden times and now, on the day when the moon is but a sliver in the sky, Jewish women welcome the rest from their work. They share food and laughter and dance, and think of the Holy One, Who cannot be found in the carved idols of the human hand and mind, but on a mountaintop amidst the clouds. And in the words etched once and then again by fire into the holy tablets.

A DIFFERENT STORY

It is traditional to give food and money to those in need before each of the Jewish holidays, Hanukkah included. And so there is a story in this collection to illustrate this very important theme in Jewish life.

This story takes place in Eastern Europe and shows that the concept of **tzedakah** *includes not only giving money and food but giving kindness as well. This related aspect of charity is called* **gemilut hasadim,** *acts of loving kindness. In this story, Reb Aaron gives the rabbis not only food but a bed by the stove and a warm welcome, while everyone else in the town ignores them. And the rabbis remember these kindnesses when they become famous.*

Both Elimelech and his brother Zusya were rabbis. Both were very wise and learned.

When the two brothers were young and not yet known for their learning, they were very poor. They had to travel by foot along the long and dusty roads when they traveled to the various villages to teach in the study halls and in the synagogues. Often they did not know where they would sleep or what they would eat.

They knew, however, that whenever they came to the town of Ludmir, they would not have to worry. Though no one else would house them, Reb Aaron, a poor tailor, would greet them warmly and take them into his home. The hot soup and black bread he fed them tasted as good as the fanciest banquet after their journey, and the beds he made them of straw and blankets by the stove felt as welcoming as a count's thick feather bed.

As the years passed, the two rabbis became famous throughout Poland for their learning and wisdom. Now they did not travel from town to town very often anymore. They did not have to. People came from all over to them, to hear the words of wisdom from their mouths and to study at their feet. When the rabbis did travel, though, they no longer went by foot, but in a fine carriage pulled by handsome horses.

One day Rabbi Elimelech and his brother Rabbi Zusya decided to return to the town of Ludmir, since they had not visited there in many years.

After traveling down the long and dusty road in their fine carriage, they arrived in Ludmir to find that all the townspeople had come to meet them. What a welcome! Surely very different from years past.

The wealthiest man in all Ludmir, Reb Joshua, even gave a nice speech and invited the rabbis to stay at his home, saying it would be the greatest honor of his life.

Rabbi Elimelech listened with only half an ear, however. He was searching among the faces in the crowd for their old friend, Reb Aaron the tailor. He smiled when he saw him.

"Thank you for your generous offer, Reb Joshua," said Rabbi Elimelech. "But we look forward to staying with Reb Aaron, if he will have us."

"What! Reb Aaron!" shouted Reb Joshua. "Why he barely has enough food to feed his own family. And he certainly does not have any extra beds for you to sleep on."

"We can eat whatever Reb Aaron offers us and sleep by his stove as we did in years past," answered Rabbi Elimelech. "When we were poor and not so well known as we are now, it was Reb Aaron who saw to our comfort. Now we, the very same rabbis, arrive in a fine carriage drawn by handsome horses and the whole town comes out to greet us. What a different story it is.

"I think it must really be our fine carriage and handsome horses that you welcome rather than us. So please, since you think so much of our carriage and horses, take them to your splendid house and show them your fine hospitality. We will go to our old friend Reb Aaron's."

And with these words, Rabbi Elimelech put the horses' reins into a surprised Reb Joshua's hands. He went off to the tailor's small but cheery home with his brother Rabbi Zusya who, though as surprised as Reb Joshua, couldn't help but smile.

REMEMBERING RIVKA

Rededication is a major theme of Hanukkah. It was on the first Hanukkah that Judah Maccabee and his army recaptured Jerusalem from the Syrians, and cleansed and rededicated the Temple to the service of God.

In this original contemporary story, "Remembering Rivka," a group of twelve- and thirteen-year-olds are moved by an older woman's sharing of her memories about the Holocaust, and decide to rescue and rededicate a Torah that was confiscated by the Nazis.

Although this story is fiction, it is still possible to "rescue" Torah scrolls that were confiscated during the Holocaust, through the Memorial Scrolls Trust in London, England.

Another example of a contemporary rededication effort is the cleansing and rebuilding of the Eldridge Street Synagogue in New York City. This, the oldest Eastern European synagogue on the Lower East Side, built in 1887, had fallen into disrepair. It is now being rebuilt through the efforts of hundreds of people who donate money and form work parties.

Stories like these show how we can continue to do as the Maccabees did—to clean, restore, and make holy the sacred objects and spaces in our lives—and find meaning, as they did, in this process of rededication.

It was Leah's bat mitzvah year, the year she and the others in her Hebrew school class would learn to lead the synagogue service and read directly from the holy scroll, the Torah. The year they would become Jewish adults. She and her classmates also had to perform *mitzvot*, good deeds—like visiting the sick, collecting food for the needy, honoring their parents.

Her parents were making good use of this.

"You don't have to do something big, Leah," her mother said. "Just keep your room clean. That's honoring your parents."

"Better a little idea with follow-through than a big one that never sees the light," her father said.

Leah winced. She knew her father was thinking of her dog-walking service. She had never gotten past her very first job with the fox terrier who bit everything in sight, including her leg. And of the exercise program with the ten-pound weights and videotape that were gathering dust by her bed.

"I get the point, Dad," Leah said.

Would anyone really consider her an adult in the Jewish community after her bat mitzvah ceremony? *Unlikely*, she thought. *They certainly don't give me much credit now, just a few months away from the big day. Just what do they expect to happen in a few months? And anyway, my ideas aren't so bad. I can't help it if things don't always work out.*

Now, a few days later, she was sitting in Hebrew school class listening to Mrs. Friedman announce the guest speaker.

You had to give Mrs. Friedman credit, Leah thought. She tried to make Hebrew school interesting.

Leah looked around at her classmates—Avi with his head shaved, Sarah chewing loudly on a big wad of gum, David rocking back and forth in his chair. He always fell over at least twice each class. The boys were both going to be Jewish adults when they turned thirteen, the girls, when they turned twelve. *What a joke,* Leah thought.

She felt sorry for the speaker. The woman looked nice enough sitting there in the front of the room, her gray hair neatly combed, her hands in her lap.

Please, David, Leah thought, *don't make any of your weird noises.*

The visitor's name was Mrs. Oberman. She was a Holocaust survivor. Leah had never heard a survivor speak. Probably none of the class had.

They were quiet, except for David's rocking back and forth, back and forth.

"I grew up in a city called Lublin," Mrs. Oberman began. "I went to a public school, had lots of friends and a wonderful family."

David still rocked, but Mrs. Oberman didn't seem to hear.

"My best friend in the neighborhood," she continued, "was Rivka, and we did everything together. Rivka was the one with the ideas. She loved to joke around and play little tricks. I was usually the one who would be discovered and get into trouble, though." Mrs. Oberman smiled, remembering.

"What kind of trouble?" David stopped rocking, interested for once.

"Well, one time, we were supposed to be studying for our exams—it was the end of the year—and Rivka talked me into sneaking off to see the little traveling circus. My parents found us. It wasn't hard. Rivka was dancing with the circus bear in the middle of a big crowd of people all clapping and laughing. That time we both got caught."

Then Mrs. Oberman's smile disappeared. "But all that changed when the Nazi soldiers came. That's why Mrs. Friedman asked me to come today—to tell you this part of my story." Mrs. Oberman paused and took a deep breath. "They rounded all the Jews up, the Nazis did, and forced us to live in a small section of the city called a ghetto. We had very little food to eat and people were taken away, one by one—we didn't know where. You can imagine how we felt. Terrified of we didn't know what.

"Well, Rivka couldn't stand it. You know Rivka. She had to do something. She got forged papers for herself—and for me, too— from a friend who smuggled things into the ghetto, and we escaped through the sewers."

Mrs. Oberman stopped for a second and closed her eyes.

I hope she's okay, Leah thought. *This must be so hard for her to talk about.*

Leah looked around. Everyone was quiet, waiting. Even David.

"Please forgive me," said Mrs. Oberman. "I've never talked about this to a whole group before." She waved her hand toward the class.

"Anyway, we got out and onto a train. We didn't know where we were going. Just away. But at one of the stops—when the Nazi soldiers got on the train and asked to see our papers—Rivka didn't have hers. Somewhere, in the running, she had lost them. They took her away and after that I . . . I never saw her again." Mrs. Oberman's voice grew a little shaky. She stopped talking again. No one said a word.

"But I was lucky," she went on. "When I got off the train, I found my way into a forest where others were hiding. And that's how I survived the war. In that forest."

Mrs. Oberman stood up. "Oh, no. Class is almost over and there are still some slides I want to show you."

Leah had seen some of the slides before. One was of a group of people being led away from the burning Warsaw Ghetto, their hands up in the air. The last one showed shelves and shelves of Torah scrolls in a warehouse, all lined up one after the other. Each Torah was labeled with a tag, a number.

"The Nazis put those tags on the Torahs," said Mrs. Oberman. "They were going to make them part of an exhibit in their museum of extinct races. I decided to show this slide last, to remind us that there is no museum and we are still here."

Over the next few days, Leah couldn't get Mrs. Oberman's story out of her mind. Or the slides, especially the last one of the lined-up Torah scrolls. Leah had never seen Torahs treated like that. In her synagogue, the holy scrolls were dressed in velvet and silver. They were carried respectfully around the congregation during services, so everyone could reach out with prayer shawls or prayer books and touch them lovingly as they went by. *Torahs should never be lined up like that, on shelves, with tags,* Leah thought.

She was still thinking of the slides when she sat in Hebrew school class a few days later. Mrs. Friedman was going on about their class project. Besides their individual *mitzvot*, they had to do something as a group.

That sure won't be easy. Not with this group, thought Leah.

"The idea," Mrs. Friedman was saying, "is to do something not just to benefit yourselves but for the whole community, and to work on it together. Last year's class collected canned food outside the supermarket for the homeless shelter. And the year before that, they wrote a play and performed it for the people in a nursing home."

David groaned loudly.

"We have enough projects to do in regular school," put in Sarah.

"But you can't save a Torah in regular school," blurted out Leah without stopping to think.

Oh, no. She'd done it again. She could almost hear her dad in the background saying, "Big ideas, little follow-through."

"What was that?" asked Mrs. Friedman.

"Oh, nothing," murmured Leah, embarrassed.

Now Sarah was looking at her. And David, too. Not that she cared.

"You said something about saving a Torah." Mrs. Friedman was being encouraging.

"It's just that I've been thinking about that slide Mrs. Oberman showed. The one with all the Torahs lined up on shelves. And wishing we could bring even one here. You know, save at least one." Leah's voice faltered.

"Go on," said Mrs. Friedman.

"It's probably just a crazy idea," said Leah. "My parents say I'm full of big ideas. But if we could find out where to get one of those

Torahs and bring it here, we could rip the tag off and read from it when we lead the service, when we come of age. Then we could put it in the Ark with all the other Torahs. That's where it belongs, not on a shelf."

Leah slumped down in her chair. What a fool she'd made of herself this time. Her father was right. This idea would never work out. Kids like David and Sarah didn't care a bit about a Torah. They'd laugh at her.

But they didn't. No one laughed.

David was the first one to break the silence. "I've been thinking about Mrs. Oberman, too," he said quietly. "And her friend Rivka. Wishing there was something I could do."

Leah was shocked. Could this really be David talking? She looked over at him. He smiled back at her. This was certainly a different David from the old chair-rocking David.

"If we could bring a Torah here," David continued, "maybe we could dedicate it to Rivka. We could embroider her name on the velvet mantle and say *In Memory of Rivka*. We could tell her story to the congregation. That way, she would never be forgotten."

All of a sudden everyone in the class began talking at once—how they would find out about the Torah scrolls and how they would raise the money to bring one here. Everyone was excited, including Mrs. Friedman, who waved her hands around in the air and beamed at them.

Leah had the feeling that this time her big idea would see the light. It would take a lot of work, but together David and Sarah, Mrs. Friedman, she, and the others would save a Torah from those shelves and bring it to their synagogue to dedicate in Rivka's memory. They could even invite Mrs. Oberman and have the dedication in time for Hanukkah, the holiday of rededication.

Wouldn't her parents be surprised! Leah smiled at the thought. She realized maybe she had been wrong after all. Maybe a lot could happen in a few months—the few months before her big day.

SOURCES OF THE STORIES

INTRODUCTIONS. Sources include *The Biblical and Historical Background of Jewish Customs and Ceremonies* by Abraham P. Bloch, New York: KTAV Publishing House, 1980; *Festivals of the Jewish Year* by Theodor H. Gaster, New York: William Morrow & Co., 1978; *The Jewish Festivals* by Hayyim Schauss, New York: Schocken Books, 1962; *The Jewish Holidays* by Michael Strassfeld, New York: Harper & Row, 1985.

DAY BY DAY (Afghanistan). Based on versions in the Israel Folktale Archives (IFA) 412, recorded by Zvulun Kort, as heard in Afghanistan in his youth, English translation by Gene Baharav in *Folktales of Israel* edited by Dov Noy, Chicago: The University of Chicago Press, 1963; *Gates to the Old City* translated by Raphael Patai, Northvale, N.J.: Jason Aronson, 1988; and *The Classic Tales* by Ellen Frankel, Northvale, N.J.: Jason Aronson, 1989.

AN EXTRA TWELVE (Israel). Based on versions in *Mimekor Yisrael: Classical Jewish Folktales* collected by Micha Joseph Bin Gorion, edited by Emanuel Bin Gorion, translated by I. M. Lask, Bloomington: Indiana University Press, 1976; *Time for My Soul* by Annette and Eugene Labovitz, Northvale, N.J.: Jason Aronson, 1987; and a version told by Rabbi Zalman Schachter-Shalomi.

LIFE IS LIKE A DREIDEL (Eastern Europe). Based on versions of the story "The Little Hanukkah Lamp" by I. L. Peretz found in *A Treasury of Jewish Humor* translated from the Yiddish by Nathan Ausubel, New York: Doubleday & Co., 1951; *The Hanukkah Anthology* edited by Phillip Goodman, Philadelphia: The Jewish Publication Society of America, 1976; *Seven Good Years and Other Stories of I. L. Peretz* translated and adapted by Esther Hautzig, Philadelphia: Jewish Publication Society of America, 1984. Barbara Diamond Goldin has added the dreidel image because the story is so much about how our lives twist and turn like a dreidel's spin, and she has changed the perspective of the story so it is from a child's viewpoint.

THE RIVER OF TORAH (Babylonian Talmud). Based on *Berahot* 61b, translated by Rabbi I. Epstein, London: Soncino, 1938.

SHALOM / SALAM (Israel). This is an original story by Barbara Diamond Goldin. Many thanks to Sadek Shweiki, an Arab college student from Jerusalem who is majoring in psychology and international communication and is especially interested in working with victims of political violence, and to Mary, Herb, Carrie, and Laila Bernstein who were his first host family in the United States. Also, thanks to Sharon Burde of Neve Shalom Wahat al-Salam, 121 Sixth Ave., Suite 502, New York, NY 10013, and to Karen Wald Cohen of Interns for Peace, 165 E. 56th St., New York, NY 10022, who all provided invaluable background information.

THE WOMEN'S REWARD (Biblical). Based on *The Legends of the Jews*, vol. 3, by Louis Ginzberg, Philadelphia: Jewish Publication Society of America, 1987; *Midrash Rabbah* Numbers 21:10 translated by Rabbi H. Freedman, New York: Soncino, 1983; *Pirke de Rabbi Eliezer*, chapter 45, translated by G. Friedlander, New York: Herman Press, 1965.

A DIFFERENT STORY (Eastern Europe). Based on versions in *My Brother's Keeper*, vol. 2, by Rabbi Naftoli Gottlieb, translated by Uri Kaploun, New York: CIS Publishers, 1989; *Souls on Fire* by Elie Wiesel, New York: Summit Books, 1972; *A Treasury of Jewish Folklore* edited by Nathan Ausubel, New York: Crown Publishers, 1965.

REMEMBERING RIVKA (United States). This is an original story by Barbara Diamond Goldin. It was inspired by a talk given by Nina Morecki, a Holocaust survivor and a very brave woman. The address for the Eldridge Street Project is 12 Eldridge Street, New York, N.Y. 10002, and for the Memorial Scrolls Trust (which lends but does not sell Torah scrolls rescued from Prague), Kent House, Rutland Gardens, London, England SW7 1BX.